HUSH, LITTLE DRAGON

To Andrew & Aidan

Boni Ashburn

BY BONI ASHBURN

ILLUSTRATED BY KELLY MURPHY

ABRAMS BOOKS FOR YOUNG READERS, NEW YORK

The illustrations in this book were made with
acrylic, oil, and gel medium on paper.

Library of Congress Cataloging-in-Publication Data:

Ashburn, Boni.
Hush, little dragon / by Boni Ashburn ; illustrated by Kelly Murphy.
p. cm.
Summary: In this variation on an old lullaby, a mother dragon promises her fussy baby a
variety of tasty treats, from a princess and some knights, to a magician and three musketeers.
ISBN-13: 978-0-8109-9491-1 (hardcover w/jkt.)
[1. Dragons—Fiction. 2. Mother and child—Fiction. 3.
Humorous stories. 4. Stories in rhyme.] I. Murphy, Kelly, 1977– ill. II. Title.
PZ8.3.A737Hu 2008
[E]—dc22
2007013120

Book design by Chad W. Beckerman

Printed and bound in China
10 9 8 7 6 5 4 3 2 1

HNA
harry n. abrams, inc.
a subsidiary of La Martinière Groupe

115 West 18th Street
New York, NY 10011
www.hnabooks.com

For my little dragons,
Henry, Jack, and Lily,
and my not-so-little-anymore dragon,
Britni
—BA

To a knight in shining armor, TJM
—KM

Hush, little dragon, don't make a sound.

Mama's gonna bring you a princess she found.

If that princess runs from you,

Mama's gonna bring you a knight or two.

And if those knights should try to flee,

Mama's gonna get a bit fiery.

When you want more goodies to munch,

Mama's gonna bring you a king for lunch.

If that king should sneak away,

Mama will find you a new entrée.

Here she comes with a fresh magician.

Don't mind the taste—he's good nutrition!

When that magician disappears,

Mama's gonna find three musketeers.

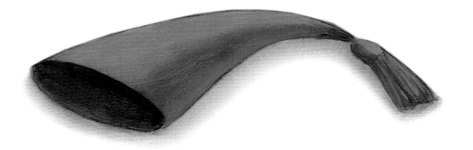

If those musketeers should bolt,

Mama's gonna stop their silly revolt.

If Mama finds a mean old queen,

Honey, you are lucky—that's good cuisine!

But if we hear a battle cry,

Mama's gonna fly into the evening sky.

"Sweet little dragon, you've eaten a ton—
Your tummy is full, you must be done!

Stars are out, let's count each one . . ."

As Mama cuddles close with her darling son.

Hush, little dragon, don't take fright.

Mama will protect you through the night.

She'll keep you snug and hold you tight.

She'll whisper in your ear, "Sweet dreams, good night . . ."